BLOOM OF JELLYFISH

SHIVER OF SHARKS

FEVER OF STINGRAYS

BALE OF TURTLES

To the Kids of Casa Hogar
Para los Niños de Casa Hogar

Shiver
Copyright © 2017 by Melissa M. Williams. All rights reserved.
ISBN 978-1-941515-75-4
Library of Congress Control Number: 2016916797

Published by Long Tale Publishing
www.LongTalePublishing.com
6824 Long Drive Houston, Texas 77087

Illustrations by Ryan Shaw with Demacio Johnson
Ocean scenes by Depositphotos.com © Natuska, ©Marylia, ©Valentinash
Design by Monica Thomas for TLC Graphics, www.TLCGraphics.com
In-house Editor: Sharon Wilkerson

First Edition
Printed in Canada.

SHIVER

BY MELISSA M. WILLIAMS

Illustrated by Ryan Shaw with Demacio Johnson

Adaptación/Adaptation by Amy R Gándara

Deep below the Arch of Cabo San Lucas, the ocean buzzed with fish families. Schools of fish swam together, dolphin pods flipped around and fevers of stingrays playfully sword fought with their siblings.

En el fondo del Arco de Cabo San Lucas, el mar zumbaba con familias de peces. Los bancos de peces nadaban juntos, mientras las vainas de delfines saltaban y los rebaños de rayas venenosas jugaban un juego de espaditas con sus hermanos.

Trevor was a tiger shark pup. He swam alone. Every morning at 8 o'clock, Trevor woke up to watch the school of clownfish swim to class. The clownfish were always in good moods, joking around with each other. He wished he belonged to a group like all of the other fish in the ocean.

Trevor era un tiburón tigre pequeño. Él nadaba solito. Todas las mañanas, a las ocho, Trevor se despertaba para ver los bancos de peces payasos que pasaban nadando. Los peces payasos siempre estaban contentos y siempre jugaban juntos. Él deseaba tener un grupo como todos los otros peces del mar.

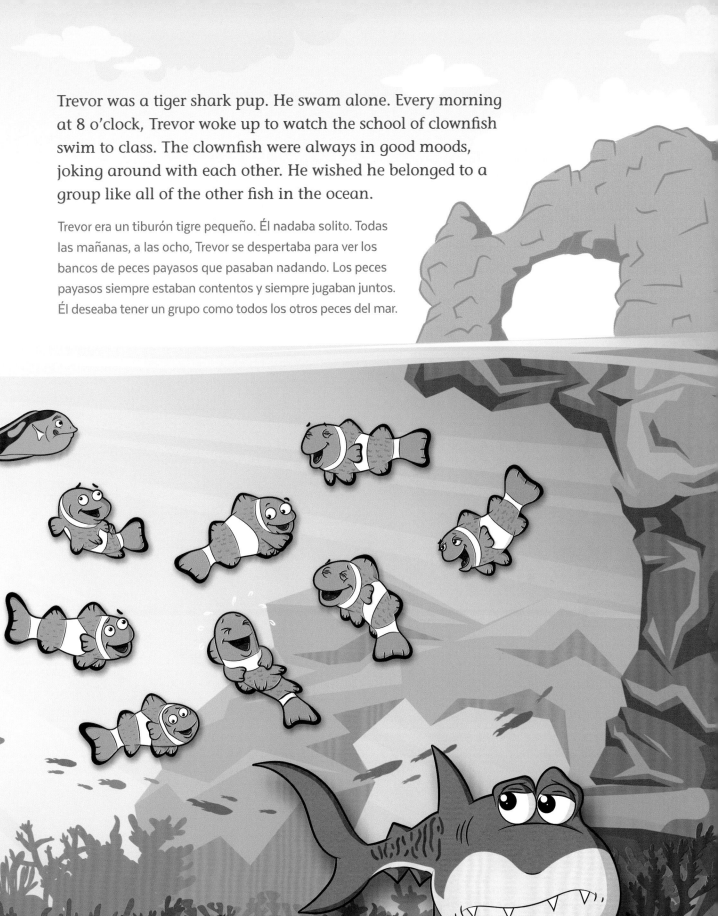

Once Trevor even tried to befriend a pod of dolphins by camouflaging his stripes.

The dolphins weren't fooled. They knew he was a shark.

Trevor hasta quiso serse amigos con una vaina de delfines y quiso camuflajearse sus rayas.

Los delfines no le creían. Sabían que era un tiburón.

"He's going to eat us!"

"I don't eat dolphins! I'm just like you," Trevor sighed.

"¡Nos va a comer!"

"¡Yo no como delfines! Soy igual que Uds.," Trevor suspiró.

Trevor swam down to the bottom of the ocean so no one would see his tears. Nearby, a stinky eel slithered out of his dark cave and over to Trevor. "Your problems can't be that bad, pup," the eel said.

Trevor glanced up at the slimy creature and asked, "Who are you?"

The eel smirked. "You don't know who I am? I'm Roberto."

"No, I don't know you. Just go away." Trevor started to cry.

Trevor nadó hasta el fondo del mar para que nadie le pudiera ver sus lágrimas. Cerca de Trevor, una anguila apestosa se deslizó fuera de su cueva oscura. "Tus problemas no pueden ser tantos, chiquitín," dijo la anguila.

Trevor miró a la criatura viscosa y le preguntó, "¿Quién eres tú?"

La anguila sonrió desdeñosamente, "¿No me conoces? Soy Roberto."

"No, no te conozco. Déjame en paz." Trevor empezó a llorar.

"Well, not until I find out why a tiger shark is acting like a baby," Roberto said and let out a long over-exaggerated hiss.

"No me voy hasta que me digas porque un tiburón tigre está de chillón," Roberto dijo y, al mismo tiempo, hizo un silbido largo y muy exagerado.

"I just…" Trevor blew out some bubbles. "I just want to belong to a pod, or a school or even a bale."

"You're not a dolphin, so forget the pod. Or a fish, so don't even think about a school. And you are definitely not a turtle, so you're bale out of luck kid. You're a SHARK! But let's get real, most sharks don't swim in a shiver anyway."

"Solo…" Trevor sopló algunas burbujas. "Yo solo quiero pertenecer a un banco de peces o una vaina de delfines o algún grupo."

"No eres un delfín, así es que olvídate de la vaina. O un pez, así es que ni pienses de un banco. Y, sin duda, no eres una tortuga, así es que olvídate de este grupo también, chiquitín. ¡Eres un TIBURÓN! Pero, de todos modos, la mayoría de tiburones no nadan en una manada."

"A shiver? What's a shiver?"

"A group of sharks. Duh."

"How can I get a shiver?"

"You can't. Of course you are all alone. I've never met a shark with a family. You guys eat everyone."

"Why are you all alone? Where's your bale or whatever?"

"Eels have swarms! Honestly, I despise anything with small brains, so that's pretty much anyone with gills. I prefer being alone."

"¿Una manada? ¿Qué es una manada?"

"Una manada es un grupo de tiburones, ¿en serio?"

"¿Cómo puedo pertenecer a una manada de tiburones?"

"No puedes porque estás solito. Yo no conozco a ningún tiburón que tiene una familia. ¡Uds. comen a todos!"

"¿Y, por qué estás solo tú? ¿Dónde está tu banco o lo que sea?"

"¡Las anguilas pertenecen a los enjambres! Honestamente, despreció a todos con cerebro chico, y así son casi todos con branquias. Yo prefiero estar solo."

"Fine, I'll leave you alone then." Trevor swam away. "You smell like a rotten egg anyway," Trevor said under his breath.

"Bueno pues, te dejo solo." Trevor se fue nadando. "Hueles muy mal de cualquier manera," Trevor habló en voz baja.

On the other side of the Arch, a young sea turtle was caught inside a jellyfish bloom. Struggling not to be stung, she yelled for help.

"HELP! HELP! I'M STUCK!" cried the little sea turtle.

Trevor perked up when he heard the cry. He immediately swam toward the sound. "Where are you? Who are you?" he asked.

"Help! I'm stuck!"

Del otro lado del Arco, una tortuga pequeña estaba atrapada dentro de una floración de aguamalas. Luchando desesperadamente para soltarse, gritó por ayuda.

"¡AYÚDAME, AYÚDAME! ¡ESTOY ATRAPADA!" gritó la tortuga pequeña.

Esto le llamó mucha la atención cuando oyó el grito. Inmediatamente, Trevor nadó hacia en dirección del sonido. "¿Dónde estás? ¿Quién eres?" le preguntó.

"¡Ayúdame! ¡Estoy atrapada!"

"I can't see you," Trevor said. "The jellyfish are too thick." The tiger shark tried to swim closer. "The tops don't sting, only the tentacles. Try slipping through the spaces."

"Oh, good idea!" Sophia the turtle carefully slid on the tops of the jellyfish until she came out of the bottom of the bloom. Trevor was there, waiting for her.

"No te puedo ver," le dijo Trevor. "Hay muchas aguamalas." El tiburón tigre quiso acercarse. "Las partes de arriba no te pican, solo los tentáculos. Trata de meterte por los espacios."

"¡Sí, buena idea!" Sophia la tortuga se fue resbalando con cuidado por las partes de arriba de las aguamalas hasta que salió por la parte de abajo de la floración. Trevor ahí estaba, esperándola.

"Arghh! You're a shark?!"
The tiny turtle swam backwards. "You tricked me!"

"¡Híjole! ¡Eres un tiburón!"
La tortuguita nadó hacia atrás. "¡Me engañaste!"

"Wait. I'm not going to eat you.
I don't eat turtles."

Sophia froze. "You don't?"

"No," Trevor said. "I only eat plants."

"Why? You're a shark."

"If I eat you, then you'll be gone. And I'll
be all alone…again."

"I know how you feel. All of my brothers
and sisters swam away after we were born
up on the beach. I don't blame them. We
were all running away from the seagulls."

"Yeah, I'm pretty sure my dad ate one of my
sisters," Trevor said.

"OMG! Rude."

"Well, he *was a* shark." The tiger shark winked.
"My name is Trevor by the way."

The little turtle giggled. "I'm Sophia."

"Espérate. No te voy a comer. No como tortugas."

Sophia se quedó inmóvil. "¿No?"

"No," Trevor le dijo. "Yo solo como plantas."

"¿Por qué? Eres un tiburón."

"Si yo te como, no estarás aquí. Y estaré solito . . . otra vez."

"Yo te entiendo. Todos mis hermanos se fueron nadando después de que
nacimos en la playa. No los culpo. Estábamos corriendo de las gaviotas."

"Pues, estoy seguro que mi papa se comió a una de mis hermanas."

"¡Ay, Dios mío! ¡Qué bárbaro!"

"Bueno, él era un tiburón." El tiburón tigre le guiñó el ojo.
"Por cierto, me llamo Trevor."

La tortuguita se rió. "Yo soy Sophia."

From that day forward, Trevor and Sophia became best friends.
They swam together. Ate kelp together. Grew up together.

Desde aquel día, Trevor y Sophia se convirtieron en mejores amigos. Ellos nadaban
juntos. Comían kelp juntos. Crecieron juntos.

The shark and sea turtle's friendship grew stronger throughout the seasons. Trevor loved listening to Sophia talk about her dreams of starting a big family. He couldn't believe that once she had almost one hundred siblings.

Early one morning, while Trevor and Sophia were enjoying the summer sun near the surface of the ocean, the tiger shark asked his best friend, "Do you think you'll ever find any of your brothers and sisters?"

"I don't know, maybe. It doesn't really matter to me," Sophia said, eyeing a juicy looking jellyfish that was floating by.

"Well, I want to meet my sister one day. And maybe my mom and dad too."

Sophia stopped chasing the jellyfish and turned back to her friend. "Didn't you tell me your dad tried to eat you?"

"Well yeah, but he's still my family," Trevor said.

Sophia smiled. "And you're *my* family."

"Besides, when I have a shiver of my own, I won't eat any of them," Trevor said and snatched the jellyfish for Sophia. "Here you go."

"I know you won't, Trevor. You don't eat anyone."

La amistad entre el tiburón y la tortuga creció durante los años. A Trevor le encantaba escuchar a Sophia hablar de sus sueños de tener una familia grande. Él no podía creer que Sophia tenía casi cien hermanos.

En las primeras horas de la mañana, mientras Trevor y Sophia estaban gozando el sol cerca de la superficie, el tiburón tigre le preguntó a su mejor amiga, "¿Crees que algún día encontrarás algunos de tus hermanos?"

"No sé, tal vez. Realmente, no me importa," Sophia dijo, mientras miraba una aguamala jugosa que flotaba cerca.

"Bueno, yo quisiera conocer a mi hermana algún día, y tal vez a mi mamá y a papá, también."

Sophia dejó de seguir a la aguamala y volteó a su amigo. "¿Qué no me dijiste que tu papá te trató de comer?"

"Bueno sí, pero él sigue siendo mi familia," Trevor le dijo.

Sophia le sonrió. "Y tú eres mi familia."

"Ya cuando tenga mi propia manada, no me comeré a ninguno de ellos," Trevor le dijo y arrebató una de las aguamalas para Sophia. "¡Esta es para ti!"

"Yo sé que no lo harás, Trevor. Tú no comes a nadie."

The seasons passed and Trevor took Sophia's words very seriously. As her *brother*, he felt the need to look out for her and protect her. Trevor was always rescuing her from fishermen hooks, chasing away smaller sharks who wanted her for lunch, and once he had to untangle her from a plastic bag that she thought was a jellyfish.

Las estaciones pasaron y Trevor tomó las palabras de Sophia muy seriamente. Como su *hermano*, él sintió la necesidad de protegerla. Trevor siempre la estaba rescatando de los anzuelos de pescadores, persiguiendo a otros tiburones pequeños que querían comerla, y hasta una vez tuvo que desenredarla de una bolsa de plástico que había confundido por una aguamala.

One autumn morning, Trevor couldn't find Sophia, so he swam up to the surface of the water to see if she was enjoying the peaceful sunrise.

The little sea turtle was nowhere to be found, so he swam to the other side of the Arch where they first met. Still, no Sophia. Even though Sophia was an excellent hider, it wasn't like her to play hide and seek without telling him.

Una mañana del otoño, Trevor no podía encontrar a Sophia, así es que nadó a la superficie del agua para ver si ella estaba gozando el amanecer.

La tortuguita no se encontraba por ningún lado, entonces Trevor nadó al otro lado del Arco donde se conocieron por primera vez. Nada de Sophia. A pesar de que Sophia era muy buena a las escondidas, nunca jugaba sin avisarle a Trevor.

Trevor spent the entire day searching for her. By the time sunset came, he had an awful feeling in the pit of his stomach. He became nauseous as Roberto slithered up to him.

"I know where you can find your friend." Roberto the eel curled his long body around Trevor's tail fin.

"I should have known that smell was you. Where's Sophia?"

"She met someone," Roberto said mysteriously.

"What? Who?" Trevor asked.

"Another turtle."

Trevor pasó todo el día buscándola. Al atardecer, él se empezó a preocupar mucho. Sintió náusea cuando Roberto se deslizó cerca de él.

"Yo sé dónde está tu amiga." Roberto la anguila envolvió su cuerpo largo alrededor de la aleta de Trevor.

"Yo debería haber sabido que ese olor eras tú. ¿Dónde está Sophia?"

"Ella conoció a alguien," Roberto le dijo misteriosamente.

"¿Qué? ¿A quién?" Trevor le preguntó.

"A otra tortuga."

Trevor's stomach instantly dropped. He swam away from Roberto before the eel could get in another word.

As Trevor headed back to the Arch, he noticed two sea turtles swimming toward him in the distance.

"Trevor!" Sophia called out.

Trevor se quedó inmóvil. Se separó de Roberto antes de que la anguila le dijera otra palabra.

Cuando Trevor empezó a nadar hacia el Arco, se dio cuenta que dos tortugas venían nadando de lejos.

"¡Trevor!" Sophia gritó.

Trevor swam toward Sophia to get a better look at the sea turtle by her side. The shark stopped to put a few feet between himself and the newcomer. "Where were you?" Trevor asked.

"Trevor, I want you to meet Max," Sophia said.

"Hello," Trevor muttered.

"This is my brother, Trevor," Sophia told the other turtle.

"Why are you with him?" Trevor asked.

Trevor nadó hacia Sophia para ver un poco mejor a la tortuga a un lado de ella. El tiburón se separó un poco entre él mismo y el recién llegado. "¿Dónde estabas?" Trevor le pregunto.

"Trevor, quiero que conoces a Max," le dijo Sophia.

"Hola," Trevor murmuró.

"Él es mi hermano, Trevor," Sophia le dijo a la otra tortuga.

"¿Por qué estás con él?" Trevor le preguntó.

"We are heading to the beach to lay my eggs."

"You're leaving? But when will you be back?"

"I'll be back soon. Don't worry."

"But we're family. We can't leave each other. And why does he get to go?"

"Trevor, I don't think you understand. We are family for life. No matter where we go."

"But who will protect you on your swim? What if a shark tries to eat you? Or what if you get caught in one of those plastic things again?"

"You have been a great protector. You taught me how to take care of myself, so now I can start a family." Sophia gave Trevor a hug.

"Vamos a la playa para poner mis huevos."

"¿Ya te vas? ¿Pero, cuando regresarás?"

"Yo regresaré pronto. No te preocupes."

"Pero somos familia. No podemos separarnos. ¿Y, por qué va él?"

"Trevor, no creo que me entiendes. Somos familia por toda la vida, no importa adonde vayamos."

"Pero, ¿quién te va a proteger mientras nadas? ¿Y si un tiburón trata de comerte? ¿O, qué pasará si te enredas en una de esas cosas de plástico otra vez?"

"Me has protegido muy bien. Me enseñaste cómo cuidarme a mí misma, para que ahora pueda empezar una familia." Sophia le dio a Trevor un abrazo fuerte.

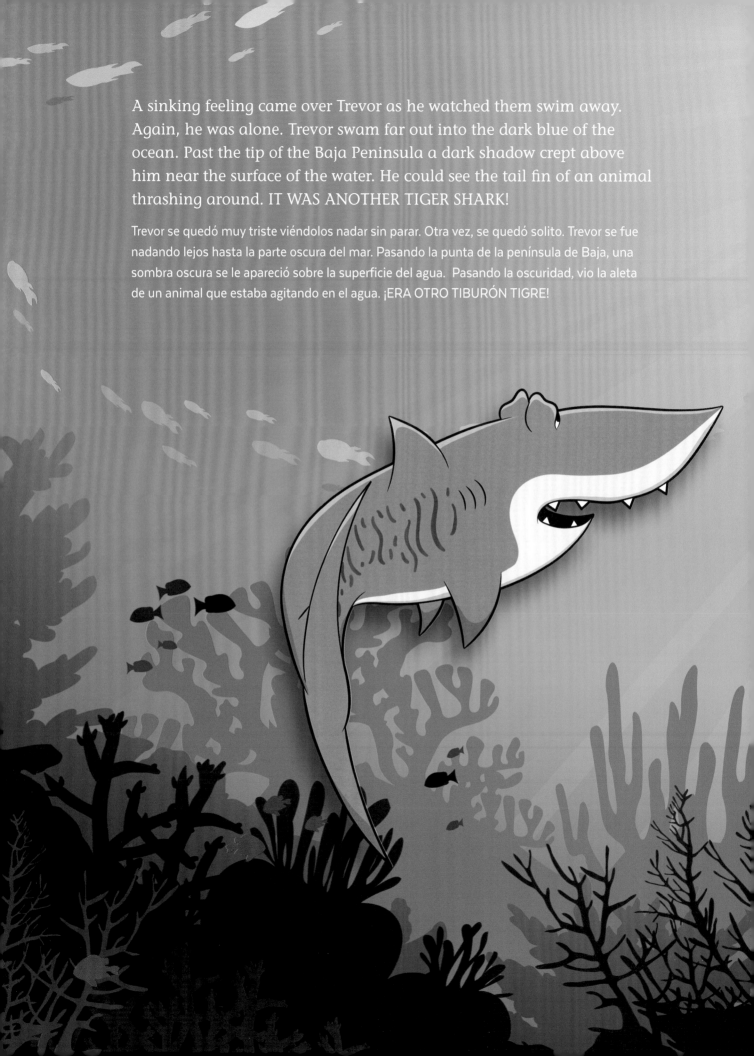

A sinking feeling came over Trevor as he watched them swim away. Again, he was alone. Trevor swam far out into the dark blue of the ocean. Past the tip of the Baja Peninsula a dark shadow crept above him near the surface of the water. He could see the tail fin of an animal thrashing around. IT WAS ANOTHER TIGER SHARK!

Trevor se quedó muy triste viéndolos nadar sin parar. Otra vez, se quedó solito. Trevor se fue nadando lejos hasta la parte oscura del mar. Pasando la punta de la península de Baja, una sombra oscura se le apareció sobre la superficie del agua. Pasando la oscuridad, vio la aleta de un animal que estaba agitando en el agua. ¡ERA OTRO TIBURÓN TIGRE!

Trevor raced to the surface to investigate. He found a young female tiger shark who was being pulled up by a fisherman's hook. Trevor had heard rumors about ships and what they do to sharks. He feared the young shark would be captured, or even worse, her fins be used for soup.

Trevor nadó rápido a la superficie para investigar. Él se encontró a otro tiburón tigre que era hembra. La estaban jalando arriba con un anzuelo. Trevor había oído rumores de barcos y lo que les hacían a los tiburones. Él tenía miedo que al otro tiburón lo capturarán, o peor, que sus aletas fueran usadas para hacer sopa.

Trevor could see the hook had pierced her lip. He knew if he pulled the hook, it could hurt her. "Don't worry, I'm going to save you," he said.

Trevor vio que el anzuelo perforó el labio de ella. Él sabía que, si jalaba el anzuelo, podría lastimarla. "No te preocupes, te voy a rescatar," él le dijo.

Trevor bolted to the surface of the water, throwing himself on the boat, mouth wide open. The fishermen jumped back in fear and let go of their prey.

Trevor se fue huyendo a la superficie del agua, se aventó arriba del barco con su boca completamente abierta. Los pescadores saltaron de puro miedo y la soltaron libre.

Trevor swam back down to look for her. He found her hiding near the reef. "Are you okay?" he asked.

"You saved me. Who are you?" she asked.

"Trevor."

"I'm Tess."

Trevor thought Tess was very pretty, even with a bloody lip. "Do you have a shiver or a family?" Trevor asked curiously.

"No, but I've always wanted one," Tess admitted. "I usually have to swim alone."

"You do? Well maybe we should start our own shiver."

Tess nodded and smiled at Trevor. Trevor vowed to never leave her side and always protect her from fishermen hooks. Tess promised to live the rest of her life with Trevor.

Trevor nadó hacia abajo para buscarla. La escondiéndose cerca del arrecife. "¿Estás bien?" le preguntó.

"Me rescataste. ¿Quién eres?" ella le preguntó.

"Trevor."

"Yo soy Tess."

A Trevor se le hizo muy bonita Tess, hasta con un labio sangriento. "¿Tienes alguna manada o familia?" Trevor le preguntó con curiosidad.

"No, pero yo siempre he querido una," Tess le comentó. "Normalmente, me toca nadar sola."

"¿En serio? Pues, tal vez deberíamos empezar nuestra propia manada."

Tess asintió con la cabeza y le sonrió a Trevor. Trevor le prometió nunca dejar su lado y siempre protegerla de los anzuelos de pescadores. Tess le prometió vivir toda su vida con él.

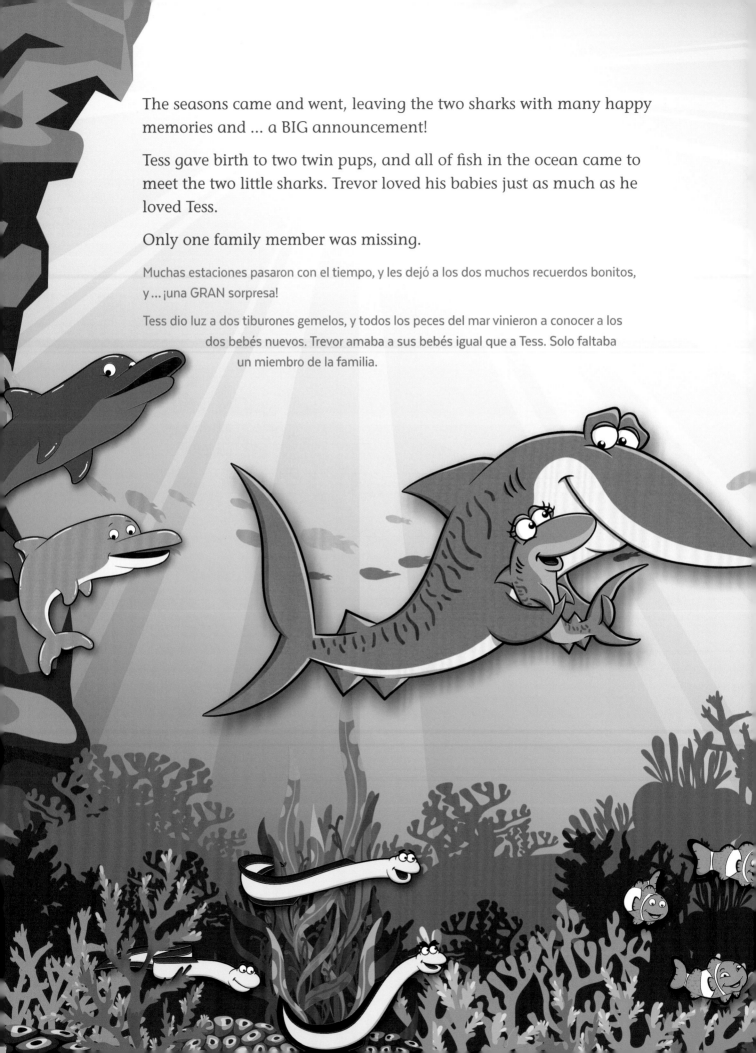

The seasons came and went, leaving the two sharks with many happy memories and ... a BIG announcement!

Tess gave birth to two twin pups, and all of fish in the ocean came to meet the two little sharks. Trevor loved his babies just as much as he loved Tess.

Only one family member was missing.

Muchas estaciones pasaron con el tiempo, y les dejó a los dos muchos recuerdos bonitos, y ... ¡una GRAN sorpresa!

Tess dio luz a dos tiburones gemelos, y todos los peces del mar vinieron a conocer a los dos bebés nuevos. Trevor amaba a sus bebés igual que a Tess. Solo faltaba un miembro de la familia.

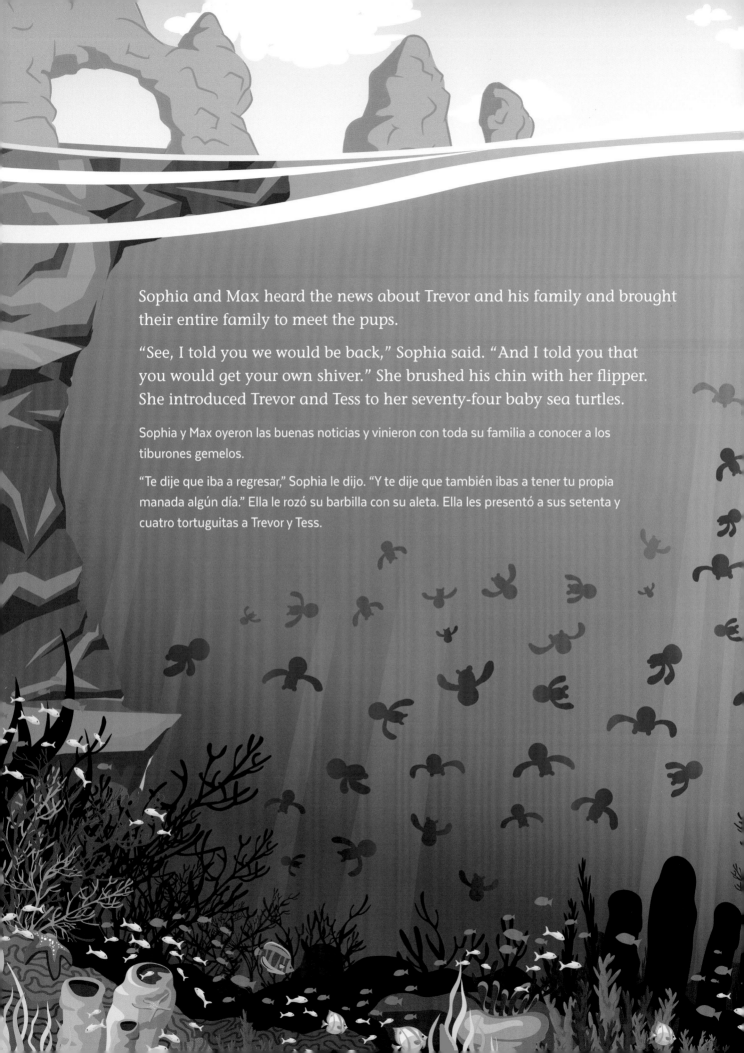

Sophia and Max heard the news about Trevor and his family and brought their entire family to meet the pups.

"See, I told you we would be back," Sophia said. "And I told you that you would get your own shiver." She brushed his chin with her flipper. She introduced Trevor and Tess to her seventy-four baby sea turtles.

Sophia y Max oyeron las buenas noticias y vinieron con toda su familia a conocer a los tiburones gemelos.

"Te dije que iba a regresar," Sophia le dijo. "Y te dije que también ibas a tener tu propia manada algún día." Ella le rozó su barbilla con su aleta. Ella les presentó a sus setenta y cuatro tortuguitas a Trevor y Tess.

From that day forward Trevor's shiver and Sophia's bale swam together, ate kelp together and grew old together. Trevor finally found his shiver and an extended bale.

Desde ese día en adelante, la manada de Trevor y la vaina de Sophia nadaban juntos, comían kelp juntos y se hicieron viejos juntos. Trevor encontró a su manada y también a una vaina.

About the Author

MELISSA WILLIAMS is an author, public speaker and literacy expert. Her first chapter book series, *Iggy the Iguana*, was released in 2008 with the *Turtle Town* chapter books and *Little Miss Molly* picture books soon following. Melissa is the founder of the iWRITE Literacy Organization and creator of the "i" The Guy comic character who focuses on getting kids to write for fun. Since 2009, her organization has published hundreds of kid authors and illustrators across the nation and hosts the annual *I Write Short Stories by Kids for Kids* Book Signing. Melissa spends the year speaking at schools and conferences, giving hands-on insight into the writing and publishing process during her creative writing presentations.

After speaking at over two hundred schools across Texas and California, she expanded her instruction to share specific creative techniques with educators. Her professional background in psychology and counseling has always been the foundation to her programs in order to get on the level of reluctant readers and writers. Melissa is a regular guest on FOX and ABC news, speaking on the need to keep reading, writing and creativity inside the home and classroom while balancing electronic usage. During her free time, Melissa can be found traveling the world studying different cultures for her next children's book.

About the Illustrators

RYAN SHAW has been drawing since he was able to pick up a pencil. He has published and illustrated his own series of "How to Draw" books, in addition to illustrating nine children's book for 4RV Publishing and LongTale Publishing. Ryan has also been a cartooning instructor at the PBS Children's Art Show held at Mark Kistler's Annual Visual and Performing Fine Arts Summer Camps held in New Mexico and Texas.

Ryan began mentoring DEMACIO JOHNSON in the world of illustrating after the young artist's work was featured on the front cover of the *I Write Short Stories by Kids for Kids* vol. 4 Anthology published by the iWRITE Literacy Organization. The two artists worked on the Shiver book project, brainstorming character ideas on Saturday mornings. Demacio became a literacy ambassador for iWRITE, sharing his experiences as an artist and writer with others. Both artists are mentors in the lives of children as they inspire them to follow their dreams and reach for the stars.

THE KIDS OF CASA HOGAR

The characters found inside *Shiver* were inspired by a group of young boys at Casa Hogar de Cabo San Lucas in Mexico. Casa Hogar houses and educates kids in need. There are times when kids are put into situations that force them to grow up faster than others, which may cause a child to feel alone. Trevor the Shark represents all kids who have felt like they didn't belong or have lost someone they loved. Through my conversations and brainstorming workshops with these incredible boys, my research companions and I found that the perception of home and family can be recreated into something everlasting. There is so much joy found in new friendships that ultimately become family.

A portion of the sale of this book will go to benefit kids in need and education programs like the Green Scholarship Program, which helps the kids of Los Cabos to achieve their dreams.

I would like to thank Patricia Pratt, Lainey & Brant Croucher, Ryan Shaw and Demacio Johnson for going on this incredible two year journey with me.

POD OF DOLPHINS

SCHOOL OF FISH

SWARM OF EELS